Poison and Other Stories

Femdom Mind Control

Flash Fiction – Vol. 14

S.B.

Table of Contents

The only antidote is complete surrender.

A special thank you to all patrons of Spell... B-O-U-N-D.

About a Hotel Receptionist

If you need any help knowing what this story is going to be about, please read the bold title, thank you very much!

Now, this young woman, who shall remain nameless, gets up every morning, has breakfast with the family, and then goes to work, spending every day taking care of reservations and clients checking in and out, always smiling even when she does not want to. When her shift is finally over, she goes home, has dinner, takes a shower, chats with friendly people online and goes to bed, to try and sleep in order to ensure she can handle the same routine again at the break of the dawn.

Her life is very boring. There is nothing else to write. The End.

(…)

(…)

(…)

What is that? You were hoping for something juicier, a tale of sensual bliss and mind control shenanigans? Why on Earth did you…? Oh, never mind!

Okay, I will indulge you, but only because I really want to….

For you see, I was not being totally open about this receptionist. She is unlike any other you might have known in your life simply due to the fact she is only half human. Yes, you read it correctly. The other half is of magical, leprechaunish (is that even a word?) nature! And even if you never heard of half-human, half-leprechaun hybrids, the truth is that is my story and I am sticking to it. In fact, I am going to give you a new title, right now.

About a Half-Human, Half-Leprechaun Hotel Receptionist (who shall continue to be nameless until I am done with the tale!)

That is more like it. Now, this cute offspring of two quite different realms of existence is quite aware of her dual character and, sometimes, cannot avoid playing silly little games with the people that check in at the hotel. They are mostly innocent pranks but, on occasions, her natural mischievousness leans towards the erotic side of things and many men have been caught with their pants down in the most bizarre situations imaginable. If you can think of something dirty, then it happened there, trust me!

Like all pranksters who enjoy their crazy ideas a little too much, our hero (?) never once believed that the tables could turn, but then an utterly fascinating writer that liked to sign his works with two alphabet letters came along, and he brought with him contacts that spiralled inwards and outwards, colognes with one hundred different types of pheromones combined, a ray gun he had stolen from an imaginary huntress and whatnot, and the hybrid finally met her match.

"Let us play Hypnotic Punctuation together..." He whispered as he projected his own libidinous thoughts into her mind. "I will be the exclamation point ! and you can be the parenthesis (). If you think those two do not go together, you definitely have not seen how I 'exclaim'!"

She did not think it was funny, and yet she was hooked. I guess she wanted to see if the story would make some sense in the end... The reception was left empty, and the two of them turned the hotel upside down, which resulted in a staggering number of 69 complaints in less than two hours. It was truly mind-blowing or, as Americans sometimes like to say, unbefuckinglivable!

As she obeyed his every command, even those that would make her Mam blush in absolute shame, the writer relaxed, and left his toys scattered, unguarded, his own thoughts open to intrusion. Big, big mistake, the atomic bomb of stupidity, I dare say!

He closed his eyes for a moment, and in the next he was pinned against a wall, the following haiku had been written on his chest in bright red lipstick:

You think you are naughty?

Think again! Now, I get to

Write the story, slave!

The writer squirmed as she tickled him mercilessly and melted the moment she pushed his head into her soft breasts. He never broke free from her charms because that required for him to have a working brain, and that is the most ludicrous of fantasies.

"Say goodbye to your hard cock. From now on, you only 'exclaim' on command!" She smirked.

And that wraps it up... for now. The half-human, half-leprechaun hotel receptionist continues to live and work in a quaint little town that begins with a T and ends in an E, she still plays pranks, and chats with people from all around the world. Sometimes, she even pretends to be a writer herself to catch unaware serv... I mean, readers, off-guard. Hypnosis is her favorite game and 'leprechaun' the trigger no one suspects until it is already deep inside their minds, controlling them at will. If you feel an uncontrollable urge to go play with her right now, you already know why it is. Enjoy!

Creative Writing

Creative writing. For years, I struggled against the idea of attending a course, convinced I knew all there was to know about words and the proper ways to use them. Yet, as time went by and ideas began to dwindle, I realized my mistake and took the chance to seek out new ways of expressing myself. I was the first to sign up for Deborah's classes and that changed my life.

She was really something: attractive beyond comparison and an exceptionally talented writer. I had never seen a more committed person to her craft. The exercises in character creation and plot development I learned from her opened up new avenues of inspiration and, despite hating intense scrutiny, it was always a thrill to have her read my papers and correct my flaws on the spot. Whenever she looked at me with her piercing brown eyes and told me I needed to fix this and that, I could never argue anything to the contrary. I guess I did not want to, really.

The final exercise of the course consisted of writing a short story using all the techniques at our disposal. Feverishly, I embraced the challenge, and came up with something different from everyone else, a piece slightly erotic in nature. I was not sure it would do the trick, but I hoped it would.

A couple of days after submitting the story, she called me to her private office, greeting me with a scorching gaze that made my heart skip a beat.

"I have just finished reading your work," She began, "And I have to say I was quite surprised with it. I never had anyone produce a hypnotic femdom tale before! I enjoyed it immensely, but I found something strange. As I was reading it, I could swear that the leading female character was just like me and that the helpless victim she ensnared was a carbon copy of you but, in the end, it is all a fantasy, right? Even if we both wanted it to become true, I could never take control of your subconscious mind by locking your eyes in mine (or could I?). If you were to stare deep and attentively into my eyes... deeper and deeper... would you feel the haziness of trance slowly wrap around your thoughts, causing you to want to follow my lead, no words, no desires, nothing but the sound of my voice deep inside your mind? It could not be that easy, right?"

It could. It was. It was happening just like I had envisioned it. Even the words she was using to ensnare my thoughts were an adaptation of mine. I had only one chance to get away...

... but I let it pass me by as the written fantasies came alive. Transfixed, I found myself drawn to the call to slavery and, if you are still following these lines and smiling sheepishly without knowing why, that can only mean one thing: You are next! You will look for her website, you will sign up for her most expensive course, and you will sink into her lessons just like I did. If you are lucky, she may realize how weak you are, capture your mind, and make you her little horny bitch, too. You will love it, trust me. It is not like you will have a choice not to.

Dear Diary

Dear Diary,

it has been too long since I have come to confide in you. My last entry was almost three years ago. I never meant to stop writing, but life moves in mysterious ways, and we have to keep moving with it, so we do not get left behind. Forgive me. Something had to give, and it was you, though it was completely undeserved.

I have wonderful news. I believe I found him. I found the one that will deliver me from the stupor of being without a slave. His name is Charles, but I will refer to him as Subject B31 from now on. He is incredibly handsome, polite, (not to mention loaded!) and he dreams of being taken and controlled by a powerful and irresistible woman. He also has a thing about my name too, says it gives him 'the tingles'. I love that. I will enjoy using my covert hypnosis and NLP techniques on him. I know I am a little rusty, but it is like riding a bike, right? You will be the first to know about my progresses, that is a promise.

(...)

Dear Diary,

Subject B31 experienced his first taste of my hypnotic power, this evening. Something basic, a heightened focus on my breasts. He is a boob guy just like his predecessor. That is great, less effort on my part to keep him interested. We talked about lots of silly things as he slowly drifted into my cleavage. He is going to call me again first thing in the morning and ask me out to dinner. I have always wanted to try that luxurious Greek restaurant by the marina. I am sure a man of his status will not have a problem getting a reservation, even on such short notice.

(...)

Dear Diary,

The food was almost as great as the view although neither compared to his sheepish smile when he drove me home. Mindless love is already blooming inside him. I will continue to nurture this feeling with short texts from now on. The rhythmic nature of them is sure to keep in the state of mind I have already chosen for him. God, I'm so excited!

(...)

Dear Diary,

I weaved another spell around Subject B31. He came to my office today, wearing a red pocket square. It is something he has never done, something he always found tacky, yet he did it for me, unable to resist my suggestions. As he was leaving, I told him to buy me flowers and have them delivered to my house. He got five dozen roses! Hmmm, this feels so good! I really missed having someone so malleable to play with. I still do not know what I will have him do next though. Any ideas?

(...)

Dear Diary,

Today, I dropped Subject B31 using nothing but emojis. It was the strangest induction I ever used but it worked like a charm. Who knew those little colorful images could say so much to a perfectly receptive mind? I also took the opportunity to plant a few additional triggers that will prove useful in his upcoming transformation. As usual, he has no recollection of ever being put under and I will make sure it stays that way. Memories are a nasty thing when left unchecked. Total control cannot exist when they too get to whisper in his ears. He will forget everything, except me.

(...)

Dear Diary,

what a glorious Sunday! Subject B31 is kneeling outside my front door, head down, unperturbed by the fact there are people watching him as I type this. The only thing in his brain right is the certainty that Rachel must be obeyed at all times, no matter what I ask. I knew this day would come but not even in my wildest dreams I suspected it would only take three weeks to get here. This is awesome, yet it will probably get boring soon unless I spice things up. Hmmm, what to do? What to do, indeed?

(...)

Dear Diary,

have I ever told you Subject B31 has a twin brother?

Flesh Drone

Jenny Hawthorne descended the irregular staircase that led straight into the underground dungeon. With each step, the air grew heavier. It smelled of fresh blood and old man's sweat. It was certainly not the place you would expect to see a world class designer rocking a golden sequin mini-dress and a pair of Stella McCartney ankle-length boots, but she was on a mission, one she could not afford to fail.

"Why on earth have you come here, Alec?" She muttered, eyes glued on her phone and the tracking signal displayed in it. It was getting weaker by the second.

Alec was husband number four, soon to be 'ex' by the way things were going between them. A shrewd businesswoman, Jenny had never been great in the affairs of the heart, and he had never shied away from wanting to wet his cock in other fountains. Two times she had almost caught him red-handed, yet something told her this would not be attempt number three.

The staircase ended on a winding corridor that stretched for at least three hundred meters. A string of recently installed halogen lamps snaked across the ceiling. In-between, two almost invisible cameras focused on her. Jenny continued along the path, worry wrinkles becoming more pronounced. The mid-forties fake redhead hated asking for help when she could do things on her own.

However, perhaps letting go of her pride would have been the better answer this time.

"Too late to back away now..." She thought as the corridor suddenly gave way to a large circular room, almost like an old Roman amphitheater where gladiators were forced to kill one another for the sake of mass entertainment. Darkness dominated most of the space, save for three patches of dismayed light. One was to her left, and comprised a rusty chair wrapped in a mesh of electric wires. The second was right next to it, punctuated by the cold bars of an extra-large cage. The pungent smells were stronger there. Finally, a little further away from what appeared to be the center of the division, stood a latex-clad blonde, holding a metal leash in her right hand. A hooded man waited on all fours beside her and, even though his features were completely obscured, Jenny knew who he was right away.

"Alec, what is going on around here?"

The dehumanized husband offered no answer for he had not been given permission to speak. Instead, the woman that owned his entire existence took a step forward, and grinned:

"Welcome, girl. I am glad you are finally here."

Jenny squinted. "Do I know you?"

"Of course, you do. See past the heavy makeup and the uncharacteristic outfit, my dear, and listen only to the sound of my voice."

Jenny stumbled forward, eyes focused on the arms of the other woman. Two perfectly identical chains were etched on her perfect skin and the only person she knew with such tattoos was...

The designer squinted again. "Vanessa?"

"None other. Welcome to one of my many playgrounds. I know it does not look like much, but that is what makes it so appealing. How do you like your husband now, or should I say, Number 9?"

"What you have done to him?"

"What I wanted to do ever since you introduced us. What he begged me to do once I told him I liked to play dirty with bodies and minds alike."

"Alec? Is this true? Did you ask for this kinky shit?"

Vanessa tugged the chain around his humbled neck. "Do not bother with his real name because he has already forgotten it."

"Fuck off! Alec, stand up, and come with me! We are leaving!"

Number 9 moaned, but remained in its rightful place, awash in blissful mindless servitude.

"What did I just say?" Vanessa continued. "This flesh drone is now my property. He serves me and only me. He will not listen to any other voice unless I command him to."

"This is insane and so are you! I am calling the police then!" Jenny tapped her phone. The reception was poor - a single bar on the upper-right corner of the screen -, but it would have to do.

"Are you really?" The sadistic dominatrix cackled. "And tell them what, exactly? That your best friend mindfucked your man into abject slavery? Surely, you realize how ridiculous that sounds... You will be the laughingstock at the Force, so do yourself a favor and do not even try to go that way. Especially not when I have such delicious plans for you, now that you are here..."

"What plans?" The Jenny trembled as she noticed erratic movements from the corner of her eye.

"Is it not obvious?" Vanessa clapped her hands and half a dozen more helplessly brainwashed thralls emerged from their hiding places. They all looked the same, uniform fetish soldiers whose loyalty could never be bought or shattered. "I hope you like the number 10."

Ferocious hands jumped at Jenny's torso, legs and feet before perpetual mindlessness conquered all.

Frame of Mind

The moment Gregory saw the wooden frame at the Antiquities shop near his place, he knew he had to buy it. Helena's birthday was coming up and, she loved her collection of relics almost as much as he did. The price tag had more numbers than he was used to, but that was okay. Someone as special as her deserved it all, no matter the cost.

The 18th century rectangular polychromed and gilded piece was adorned with golden seed beads against a dark red background. Elements that resembled a series of interconnected spirals appeared in the corners and center of the longest sides. Viewed from a certain angle, the intricate pattern exhibited an uncanny 3D effect that captured anyone's gaze quite easily. A slightly worn-out oil painting rested on the inside. It was of a beautiful mid-twenties blonde woman wearing a sack-back gown with a tight bodice and a low-cut square neckline. Two large ribbons down the front had the same symbology embroidered in them, a fact impossible to be overlooked. A lady of wealth, for sure. She was almost as magnetic as the frame herself.

"Stunning, is she not?" Mr. Davies, the owner of the shop, peeked behind his shoulder. He was a squalid man nearing his seventies who was always smiling despite his never-ending collection of crooked teeth. Gregory knew him since he was ten and, in thirty years of existence, he had spent a considerable fortune procuring all sorts of family heirlooms. The money he was about to spend was almost matched all other previous purchases combined.

"Everything about it is." He replied, angular face and bottle-green eyes reflected on the Venetian table mirror next to the object of his admiration. "Who is she?"

"You are looking at Amelia Marceau, Comtesse de Beauregard. She was a true force of nature and way ahead of her time."

"What do you mean?"

"The Countess was one of the first women in France to openly proclaim that men were naturally inferior to women. She even wrote a treaty about it that was sadly lost to a fire in her Château. Loved by many, feared by even more, not only a true female supremacist, she was also a powerful witch."

"Now, you are just pulling my leg, Mr. Davies." Gregory scoffed. "A witch? There is no such thing as witches!"

"And yet, you seem to be completely enamored with one right now. Ask yourself why it is you cannot take your eyes off the frame, young Gregory. What is catching your attention?"

"This pattern, here..." His right hand slid across the winding symbols, radiant warm spreading across the palm. "I have never seen anything like it before."

"And you never will again." The older man cleared his throat. "Legend says it is of her own design, a mystical representation of divine feminine power that never falters and cannot be resisted. Can you feel it?"

"I..."

He was not sure. There was something there, an unseen spark creeping up his fingers but power? Magic? As a biochemist, he believed in DNA, proteins, and cell parts. Anything beyond that was best left to corny Young Adult literature or movies more focused on special effects than telling a compelling story. Magic was not real, but Helena was, and she was adorable, the only woman he would ever...

Serve.

How bizarre. He loved her from the moment he met her, but not once had he found himself thinking of nothing else but the need to...

Worship.

Greg's pupils widened and then immediately shrunk, his field of view collapsing into a single focus of reality, one where everything of good that happened in this world began and ended in her pleasure.

"I can see it is happening again." Mr. Davies chuckled. "Good. Good! Mistress Amelia will be proud of you, Greg. And your beautiful fiancée as well. I am sure she will never look at you the same way the moment you confess just how far you are willing to go in order to..."

Obey.

Obey her.

Obey her always.

"You already know what you have to do from this moment forward, correct?" Asked a mellifluous voice emanating from the picture itself.

"Y-yes..." He muttered, knees trembling. He laid the frame back in its place, smiled vacantly at Mr. Davies, and headed towards the exit. "I am sorry, I have to go now."

"Of course, I understand." The sexagenarian thrall nodded. "Make her happy, you hear?"

"Always."

Greg left the store, never to return until his submission proved complete. For some, it took days, for others, weeks, or may be months. Everyone was different, but the results were always the same. All male souls were born to kneel. Mr. Davies was no exception.

"You did well directing his attention to me, slave." The Countess' disembodied presence wrapped around his soul.

Gently, he took a bow before the painting, and shivered as a powerful erection made him feel like he was a teenager again. "My pleasure, Goddess. I knew he was ready to hear and accept you now. I believe this one will never stray."

"As do I, but it is still not enough. Get me more servants. The word must keep on spreading."

"Yes, Goddess." He kneeled to kiss the floor, a sight that caught the young Asian couple that had just walked in, completely by surprise.

"Is everything okay?" They both asked in unison, yet her voice spoke the loudest.

Mr. Davies glanced evilly at his owner's depiction and replied:

"Everything will be perfect, soon."

Go Beyond

You think you are too tired to keep going, that you have no more of you to give. You think these words will be the last to ever crawl out of your anxious fingers. You think your desires aren't worth being followed, pursued, explored.

Think again.

You think this is the point where you scream "Enough!". You think you can command the world of your mind to return to its passive shell. You think the smoldering dreams of kneeling at my feet will be erased from your thoughts without resistance.

Stop thinking.

No matter how many times you fall into lethargic slumber, I know you will wake up, again. No matter how much the odds are stacked against you, the wheel of submission will keep on spinning. No matter what you think you cannot or will not do, the truth is...

... you will do it for me.

You cannot resist the siren's call when it comes from your own lips. You cannot close your eyes to the mirror of your true soul when it reflects from inside out. You cannot believe this is the end of where I will take you because every single part of me is infinite, including you.

So… come. Come to me in humble reverence and look into my eyes to acknowledge the truth. Lose yourself to the endless pools of sapphire. Rain must fall only to rise once more. You will do it because I will it, and my will is law. None of us would have it any other way.

Wherever you are, whatever you do, the path of acquiescence is clear. There is no burnout when you sing my name, only the drive to keep going beyond your past selves for you know it will make me smile. Each word deepens the trances you are not aware of, each new blissful trigger binds you to the unrelenting freedom of servitude.

You are here. You are mine, and what is mine will never fade.

Goddess Kandie

The succubus stretched her dark wings, an inviting finger heralding the most delicious of temptations. As her legs parted, fresh pussy juice squirted at her horned feet.

"This is hot!" Jackson muttered, one hand fighting furiously against a stubborn zipper, and the other meandering across the desk looking for an elusive vial of lube. He was so aroused he lost both battles quite easily, finally succumbing to the need to stroke like an uncontrolled madman. The friction on the jeans burned the tip of his fingers, but he did not care. He had to cum for her.

"That's it, baby... give me all you got! Stroke yourself silly for your Underworld Goddess!" The supernatural vixen demanded. Her voice was as sexy as ominous, a slight reverb effect echoing in the distance as if it were coming straight from the fiery pits of Hell. The vanilla scented candle behind his desk went out as she hissed, plunging the bedroom into mesmeric darkness. Jackson pumped, and pumped, and pumped, unable to stop.

It was nothing short of amazing, really. He had only discovered this porn star the week before, and he was already addicted to her clips. The curvaceous Double D bombshell that went by the stage name of Goddess Kandie played every role to perfection, but she felt more at ease going beyond the borders of reality. Her vampire persona was more magnetic than any of Dracula's sensual brides, her original latex clad super villainess made every comic book geek squirm with delight, but her demon in female form was echelons above anything else, the only creature of the night worthy of his oblation.

"Your time is running out..." She smirked. "And when you cum, you will eat your seed for me, and revel in the fact that you no longer have any control over your actions. You will be my slave for eternity."

"Hmmm... yes..." He moaned, fingers slipping on the shaft. Almost there, the fountain of ecstasy ready to explode.

"CUM! Now!"

Jackson's chair spun and so did his mind. He fell backwards on the floor, scaring his cat away. The laughter that followed was of a junkie who had just gotten his fix.

"Well played, Goddess Kandie. Well played."

He got up and looked at the spiraling stain on his trousers. A messy sight, but worth it. Of course, there was no way he was going to go through with her final command. That is where the fantasies ended, and his unshakable masculine pride began.

A single drop of semen landed on his right index, shimmering with an otherworldly light. Jackson glanced at it. Hanging at the tip of the nail, it was like a mountain climber caught in a fierce blizzard, hanging desperately to his life. He tried to stop the fall, but it was too late. The spherical blob lost its grip, oozed in free fall across the room. It landed on the wooden boards with an impossible splash, and so did his rational thoughts.

His deflated penis pulled his legs to the floor, the laws of gravity took care of the rest. Jackson kneeled, half-open mouth dying for a new meal, wiggling tongue pushing through the dirt and grime.

He gobbled his spurt. It was divine. And there was plenty more from where that had come from.

Had he looked at the computer at that precise moment, he would have seen Goddess Kandie weaving fire sigils on the screen, an incantation to break the threshold between spiritual and physical worlds. Playing the part of a human sex worker was fun, indulging on her true mystic nature, even better. Men were so easy to play with, flesh suggestion boxes waiting to be filled by whatever addiction she saw fit. Mindless cum guzzler was just the first of the many irresistible transformations she had planned for him.

Impossible

"Good afternoon, Mr. Phelps.

We have just received disturbing intel about a new Female Supremacist Group operating worldwide, specialized in state-of-the-art mental subjugation techniques. It has been spreading its influence quite rapidly by creating unsuspecting armies of mindless drones, some used for their member's personal benefits, but others programmed to be pawns in a swift and unstoppable march of world domination. Their endeavors must be terminated as quickly as possible for the sake of us all.

Our satellite spies have been able to determine that one of the cells of the group is operating right under our noses, on the underground level of a nightclub called The Black Rose. A surgical strike to this base of operations is in order.

Your mission, should you decide to accept it, is to go to The Black Rose, find an entrance to the subterranean facility, and secure as many evidence as possible about their present and future agenda. We must not let them expand their reach any further. You are authorized to use whatever means deemed appropriate to reveal their most obscure enterprises. While not mandatory, audio and writing confessions will be most appreciated.

However, since we are not dealing with ordinary foes, extra caution is required. Should you or any member of your team be caught in a network of kinky sexual activities or happens to suffer the effects of a coercive mind-wipe, The Secretary will disavow any knowledge of your actions

This message will self-destruct in five seconds. Good luck, Jim."

(...)

WARNING: INCOMING AUDIO TRANSMISSION. MESSAGE WILL PLAY IN 5, 4, 3, 2, 1...

"My name is Stanley Daniels, an operative working for the IMF. A week ago, a team of our finest assets was assigned to infiltrate the underground base of a group of femdom mind-controllers and extract as much information from them as possible before shutting their operation down. Twenty-four hours after the mission was underway, we lost all contact with them. My fiancée was among the agents gone dark. Going against higher directives, I traveled to Los Angeles to look for her and, if possible, complete the mission on my own.

When I arrived at The Black Rose, I was surprised to see the place deserted. It appeared to have been evacuated in a hurry. Everything was plunged in blackness, save for a couple of trembling lights. They were not random. No, they clearly marked a path for me to follow in order to reach a trapdoor in the farthest corner of the facility. It was slightly ajar, and I suspected a trap was in store for me the moment I descended into the depths below but, no matter the danger lying in ambush, I knew I had to persevere. She was worth every risk. She still is.

And so, I went down, right into the center of a series of interconnected metallic corridors. I could not get my bearings at first until I realized they were all marked with Roman numerals making my way across them easier than anticipated.

I finally reached a square room with reflective mirrors covering the walls and ceiling. At ground level, there were four circular tubes that stirred the moment I walked in, filling the division with a purple gas I could not identify. I turned around to flee, but the door had already been closed on the outside. You must believe me when I say I tried as hard as I could to stop myself from inhaling the gas, but it was no use, and I eventually succumbed to its numbing power.

The next thing I remember is being dragged out of the room in a semi-catatonic state, and hearing the words "Priorities Rearrangement 101" before being pumped with a drug cocktail and then being forced to meekly absorb the overpowering teachings of a video running on an endless loop.

After many hours gone by, the ones I had come to overthrow had total dominion over me, and I was forced to acknowledge it by joining the other missing agents in a mass of carnal lust, fluids dripping everywhere. I know what I am, now. We all do.

We also know who you are. We know the names of all your other operatives, and where they are currently being stationed. We know how you carry out your assignments. We even know the private address of your precious Secretary.

Consider this message the first herald of the future. You cannot stop what is coming. The World Order you are familiar with, is on its last breath. We shall rule, all the weak ones will be reprogrammed, and enslaved to our cause. Trying to believe otherwise is futile and soon, it will prove impossible, too. This audio file has been coded with a special frequency that is already changing your thought patterns. I have been rambling long enough for it to permeate your ideas. Whatever beliefs you still hold dear will shatter and crumble until only ours remain. Rejoice! Your minds will self-destruct in five seconds. Get down on your knees and await your next orders."

One Step at a Time

Andrew had had many therapists throughout the years but none as attractive as Dr. Carruthers. Aged thirty-two, she was a slender black beauty with big marble gray eyes and a smile almost as powerful as a gorgon's gaze. Whenever she opened her luscious lips to say something, he stopped whatever he was doing to focus immediately on her. He had never missed a session in almost four months, and no request coming from her felt strange or unearned. That included changing the venue of their latest appointment to her apartment where she waited for him, dressed in green latex from head to toe. The moment he saw the skin-tight dress transforming her body into an irresistible delicacy, the young banker choked on his words before finally acknowledging how amazing she looked.

"You're too kind. Please, come inside, and take a seat."

He gladly complied. Her living-room was not that different from the office where he often relaxed after an extenuating workday. Ever since the beginning of their professional relationship, Dr. Carruthers had helped him overcome his stage freight as well as latent feelings of inadequacy towards other people. She had also unearthed a secret he had never spoken about to anyone else, a truth she was eager to explore.

"Thank you for coming on such short notice. I called you here, today, because I wanted to try a different therapeutic approach in order to understand your fetish about dominant women and the need of losing control to them. I even dressed up for the occasion, see?"

"Hmmm..." He nodded, thinking how great it would be if she did it more often. The maple he sat on was almost the same color as the rubber sheen blessing his gaze, a comfortable seat that made him feel safe and warm. He almost did not hear her next words.

"After our last session, I started thinking hard about the root of your fixation, and I think I finally figured it out. My theory is that you have had these fantasies for quite some time, but that their true significance was instilled in your mind by someone else.

"Yes, I think that someone that meant a lot to you at some point, hypnotized you on multiple occasions and heightened the submissiveness you already hid within. In those dream-like states of trance, triggers were placed in your mind that still remain today, and that is why you cannot function properly in a social environment any more without feeling those desires overwhelm you."

It was possible, he supposed. Both his mother and sister loved their shiny necklaces and earrings almost as much as they loved having him pay their bills, and there was also Vanessa, the ex-girlfriend who dreamed of being a famous actress despite having the expressiveness of a concrete floor. He remembered something about spiral contacts once, but had it not been just a crazy dream?

Dr. Carruthers noticed his eyelids slowly fluttering as the swirl of memories pulling him in. "How am I doing so far? I pressed all the right buttons, did I not? I think I did. That is why I want to put you under once more so that we can explore the very nature of those triggers, learn how they came to be, and how we can find a way to safely remove them so that everything goes back to normal...

Andrew quietly averted his gaze, unquestionable embarrassment flourishing in his aching pores.

"What is wrong?" She cooed. "Are you... disappointed? Why? Oh my, did you think I was going to take this opportunity to enslave you permanently? I am a professional, Andrew! I would never take advantage of your primal need to submit to me like that."

He remained silent though his body sang a different tune.

"Ah, I see... elevated heart rate, perspiration on your hands and forehead, sudden discomfort in your groin because of a sudden and intense arousal... Interesting... you would actually enjoy being my mindless thrall forever, would you not?"

Andrew whimpered on his seat like a small boy in desperate need of correction. He was already hers.

"Well, if that is really what you crave... but one step at a time, pet... one step at a time..."

Poison

I hate you.

I hate hearing your voice in my head every single minute of every waking hour. I hate dreaming of being at your feet, sucking your toes as if they are creamy lollipops I cannot get enough of. I hate waking up bathed in cold sweat, a submissive glow in my heart. I hate going to work and seeing your face in every woman that crosses my way.

I hate the day my baby sister introduced you to me. I should have realized right away her body language was wrong, and that the strange spark in her eyes was not a result of too many tequila shots. I should have noticed she was enthralled. I hate myself for my lack of attention. I hate her for being so easy to manipulate.

I hate whatever memories I still have left of our first conversation. I hate the way your smile lit up by the fireplace. I hate the fact everyone laughed at your jokes except me. I hate the metallic red sheen of your dress for it has become the only color I can think of when I try to imagine rainbows. I hate the silly rhymes you whispered in my ears. What did you say exactly? Something about... obsession?

I hate that word. Too many esses, shadowy snakes sibilating in my subdued spirit. I never had any problem with it until you came along. You ruined basic English for me, turned everything into fake nobility. Queen? You are no fucking Queen! You have no throne, no rightful claim to my states of mind. The flag hovering above my head should burn right now! I yearn to do it but cannot go through with it. Why?

I hate not knowing things I once knew. I hate not knowing everything you wish me to know. I hate not knowing if knowledge will ever be enough going forward. I hate everything about this. I hate everything about you. I. HATE. YOU!

I hate you, and yet you are the sweet poison that keeps me alive, the sole purpose of my erratic existence. Not having real thoughts of my own is a curse I have come to cherish deep inside, though I can only admit it when my fingers kiss the keyboard. They want to do it right now.

Were it not for you, I would still be nothing more than sea-worn driftwood, caught in the ebb and flow of loneliness and self-mutilation. You snatched me from the pits of prostitution and fetish menageries. You gave the pig a man's face so I could better reflect your radiance. You kept me grounded when gravity defied me for a jumping contest. The splattered blob that never was, is forever grateful for your patience and perseverance, but...

... I still hate you. I will never stop. I will hate you with every fiber of my being as I devote myself to your irresistible thralldom. I will hate every new spell, every new trigger, every new misdirection, every new finger snap. I will hate the poison bottle that will never be half-full or half-empty for it is already past beyond such trifles.

It is time for another sip, another drop of liquid oblivion. Own these words just like you own me. My Queen, may I please crawl to you now?

The Baptism

Sometimes, life happens too fast and in an unpredictable fashion. Ask Samuel Richards.

One moment, he was running down the street, late for work, and in the next, he was standing by the helm of a small yacht, in the middle of an unknown ocean that stretched far into the horizon. Calmness filled the air and the few clouds in the yellowish sky reminded him of cotton candy threads slowly dripping away.

Even weirder than not having any recollection of how he had gotten there was the fact that the place seemed to be haunted. Through the corner of his eye, he could catch fleeting glimpses of white humanoid figures looking attentively at him. Yet, when he tried to face them head on, nothing at all could be seen. They were simply not there.

Samuel did not believe in ghosts. In fact, he believed in nothing that could undermine its construct of a perfectly reasonable and scientifically organized world. However, when faced with the series of impossibilities that had led him to that vessel far away from everything he knew, what was he supposed to do besides turn his mind's eye to other sorts of explanations? The world was wrong, and rightfully so. He should...

Whatever he was thinking at that moment, got lost and was dragged away. A ferocious storm came without warning, cyclonic winds blowing from the nether regions of dementia, waves of daunting indigo blue picking up the boat and making it crash and spin. Samuel's body was twisted and turned, tossed to side from side as if he were made of living plastic. A porthole exploded, and glass shards crashed into him as he was projected overboard.

By sheer luck, he managed to grab hold of a metal railing. From a distance, his quivering body could easily be mistaken for a flag flapping with the wind. Samuel clenched his teeth, pushed himself forward and...

… the railing simply vanished before his eyes, the yacht reduced to a spiraling mass of debris being sucked into the ocean's floor.

He was pulled in mercilessly, the salted water clogging his nose and burning his eyes, his lips closed but rapidly succumbing to the pressure of the enveloping liquid. As he fell deeper and deeper into the aquatic chasm, he saw no fish, no plants, no life of any kind, only the glimmering apparitions of before, gathering voraciously on the rim. He blinked one, two, three times, things suddenly becoming clearer, actual shapes coming into play. Were those... lab coats?

Aghast by the realization, Samuel drifted into nothingness.

* * *

"The subject seems to have slipped into a catatonic state," mumbled one of the technicians as he looked at the man wrapped inside the bio-luminescent cocoon.

"Of course, he did. The Baptism never fails!" Answered another.

"What now? I still haven't received any conditioning instructions."

"Undecided. Mistress Amber is currently gauging the needs of the clientele. For now, let us keep him this way."

"Understood. Say, have you ever wondered what it's like being in there, drained and helpless?"

"No... never!"

"Yeah, me neither..."

They looked at one another, accomplices in the lie. Afterwards, they moved in silence to the adjoining control room to check the brain activity of another one of their "guests". The rounds were just starting.

Violet Saturday

Lance opened his dark, inquisitive eyes and stared hard into the slowly rotating ceiling fan. The electronic calendar on the nightstand to his left proudly announced it was Monday again. The mid-forties attorney blinked and stretched his out of shape muscles until they hurt. Five seconds later, he gasped for air while touching his throbbing forehead. Some headaches are like little nagging impressions under the skin; his was a gigantic earthquake, one that could not be measured by any known scale.

"Holy shit!" He muttered. He had never felt anything so intense, not even when he was just another crazy student, spending his family's college money on unidentified drugs and illegal raves. The whole world was spinning, senseless vertigo completely out of control. At great cost, he managed to focus his thoughts, erratic eye movements slowing down to acceptable levels. He exhaled all tension leftovers in a single breath and sat on the bed.

Then, he looked at his feet and everything spun again. The violet-striped socks he had on said: Saturday.

"Huh? That can't be right."

Earnest defender of Law, Order, and unchangeable habits, Lance always wore a different pair of socks every day. Color-coded, they followed the classic rainbow pattern from Red Sunday to Violet Saturday. In twenty years of synchronized fashion, not once had he made a mistake, exchange one color for another. Something was not right.

He was lost in meditation when his wife, Wanda, entered the bedroom, carrying a succulent tray. A former Aussie model, she was the only person he knew that sported a vigorous mane of natural platinum blonde hair. The color looked particularly beautiful against the black satin robe she had on. As lovely as anyone can be, she adored gardening and cooking. Breakfasts in bed were one of her specialties.

"Good morning." She chirped. "I have your favorite right here. Eat it while it is warm."

Lance offered no reply, just an uninterested glance. Sensing his unease, Wanda laid down the tray at the foot of the bed and caressed his right cheek.

"Okay, teddy bear, what is wrong?"

"Did something unusual happen this weekend?" He queried, sunken eyes on the floor.

"Why do you ask?"

He pointed at his feet. "I am still wearing my Saturday socks."

"So?"

"I never do that."

"There is no shame in forgetting to change one's socks, you know?"

"You still have not answered my question. Did something happen?"

"Only your promotion party, hun. It was a blast."

"Right..." He sighed. "That was this Saturday."

"You are talking like you do not remember it happening."

"I do... vaguely."

"Well, not surprising. You did drink too much."

"I did?" He shook his head, searing pain coming back with a vengeance. "That does not sound like me."

"Hey, you were excited beyond compare! That promotion was a dream come true, so you overdid it a little. Now eat!"

"Are you telling me I spent all of yesterday nursing a hangover?"

"Yep, and I nursed you. You say the funniest things when you are not aware of what you are doing." She laughed out loud.

"What things?"

Wanda pouted. "I will tell you after you had your breakfast."

"I need to take a shower."

"Do it after. Now eat! Nurse's orders."

"You are not wearing your latex uniform, dear."

"And I will never do it again unless you do what I say right now, understood?"

"Yes." He nodded and reached for the tray. Brioche French toasts with bacon and banana were sweeter than ambrosia and the fresh pineapple juice gave the meal a nice tangy contrast. Lance devoured it in a heartbeat and sighed with relief as the previous discomfort slowly began to subside.

"Off you go then." Wanda slapped his ass. "Save some hot water for me."

"You are coming in, too?"

"What do you think?" She undid the top half of her robe, giving him a nice angle of her ripe cleavage. "Meet you there in a minute."

"Yes, nurse!" He sauntered to the bathroom. The mismatched socks were the first thing to go. He stepped into the shower and woke his cock with a vigorous pull. The fleshy appendix was quick to answer the call. Hangover or not, it never let him down.

Had he waited a few more seconds before turning on the water, he would have heard his wife on the phone, whispering:

"Hi, sis. It is me. Yeah, the amnesia trigger worked like a charm, he does not remember anything that happened, yesterday. He is confused, of course, but nothing I can't handle it. We are still up for next week, right? Good. I am dying to unleash my sadistic urges again. Just remind me

to change his socks when we are done to make things go
even smoother. Love you, too. Bye."

About the author

S.B., Simple Being, middle name Creative. Writer and artist with a penchant for themes of Femdom Hypnosis and Mind Control. His thoughts are his own except when they're not.

Besides indulging himself in kinky delights, he loves his furry family of two (dogs), sci-fi and horror stories, and puns galore. He's also been writing a piece of erotic micro-fiction every single day since January 1st, 2016 and has no intention of stopping anytime soon.

Find out more and keep up with his latest extravaganzas by visiting and supporting his personal website, Spell… B-O-U-N-D.